Heaven's Time

A GIFT OF CHRISTMAS

Heaven's Time

A GIFT OF CHRISTMAS

PATRICIA M. BOARDMAN

REIMAGINING HISTORY
· FOR TOMORROW ·

For information contact:
pmboardmanauthor@gmail.com

Published by:
Reimagining History for Tomorrow

Copy Editor: Kim Autrey • Content Editor: Debbie Ihler Rasmussen

Cover Illustrations by Wyvanna Hood

Cover and interior book design by Francine Platt, Eden Graphics, Inc.

Paperback ISBN 979-8-89454-029-0

eBook ISBN 979-8-89454-030-6

Library of Congress Number: Pending

Manufactured in the United States of America

First Edition

Arthur Vincent "Butch" Boardman

February 13, 1956 – October 21, 2024

"Well done thou good and faithful servant."

MATTHEW 25:21 KJV

Prologue

WHEN I SAT DOWN to author this story, I
did not know I would be writing it as my
brother was dying. Arthur (Butch) Boardman was
a year and a half younger than me. He was always
a sweet little boy, and we schemed and shared
our childhood together for four years, before the
arrival of our twin sisters. Butch was intellectually
disabled but was a fully formed person capable
of love greater than most normal people. He was
always happy, kind, and helpful to people around
him. Butch had strong faith in Christ and loved
watching movies about Jesus.

A month before he died, he asked about my
new story, and I told him I was having a tough
time getting it finished. But I promised him that I
would dedicate this short story to him and that I
would place his picture inside. His eyes lit up and

he said, 'I will be in a book?' He was so happy. I told him I would send him the first copy so he could enjoy it. Unfortunately, that was not to be, but he died knowing how much I loved him.

So many people depart around the holidays. It is particularly painful because they were making plans for those special days, wrapping gifts, or buying costumes that respectively he or she will never open or wear. These items can tear at our hearts and heap on the survivor's guilt. We feel so sad because life was interrupted. After my brother passed, I kept some of his things. It was hard but I packed up his jewelry in little plastic bags and donated them to a disabled school. They were out of prizes for bingo, and the school was so happy to get them. Those items got a new life, and another person found enjoyment with them.

During Hurricane Helene I saw the story of a woman and her seven-year-old son. Stranded, they held tree branches as their lifeline, while the torrent raged by them taking their strength with it. His dear mother could not reach him. The young son was holding smaller branches and was more vulnerable than his mom. The mother recalled in an interview, that a week earlier her son told her he wanted to be a super-hero for Halloween. But now he clung to the branches, as he cried out for to Jesus to save his life. His strength gave out and he slipped away.

I will never forget the faith and courage of that mother and son.

I authored this little story to take us outside ourselves. It is hard to do, I know. As Christians, we know that if we keep the Ten Commandments, respect the Sacramental Communion, and follow the Golden Rule, we have nothing to fear in death. Death is a rebirth, a continuation of life in the presence of God.

Faith is the main character in this story. Her mother passed away in early December. She is struggling with grief. Then she gets the opportunity to linger in the foyer of heaven on Christmas Eve. She discovers a small glimpse of what God has in store for us all. We only have to have faith and we will live in His Light forever.

Heaven's Time
A GIFT OF CHRISTMAS

MY NAME IS FAITH R. FLYNN, at least that's what it says on the cover of my books. Flynn is my mother's maiden name. I was born in Mt. Hope, Wisconsin. Four generations of my maternal line have grown up here, in the same Victorian farmhouse. My mother taught me that the pioneers who settled here wanted to create an educated, God-fearing community of people. So, they named it Mt. Hope.

Carrying a paper grocery bag, middle-aged Faith stepped out of her house. Her steamy breath turned to crystal in the December air. A click of her fob unlocked her blue sedan. She climbed inside, started the engine, and waited for the warmth of the heater to defrost the windows.

She backed out of the driveway and drove slowly down a long gravel road, through the rural village and hilly farmland.

Faith came to a Y in the road. She turned right and followed the road as it wound up a small hill. She continued past a fenced-in field with neat rows of corn stubble covered with snow. She rolled to a stop under the wrought iron arch over the entrance, with Mt. Hope Cemetery etched in the metal.

She pulled her blue sedan to a stop, exited the car, and made her way to a grey granite stone standing upright among the rows. The inscription read:

Regina O'Brien
March 1, 1938
December 6, 1999

Her nervous system on fire, Faith could barely stand. Her lip trembled as she pulled a red and green scarf from her jacket. She knelt in the snow and wrapped the scarf around the cold, hard stone.

Faith blew on her stiff hands and said quietly,

"I don't want you to be cold out here, Mom. I'm sorry I didn't spend more time with you this year. There are so many questions I want to ask you. So much I don't know about you."

Her phone buzzed in her pocket. She retrieved it, flipped it open, and pressed the green call button.

"Hello, Bernice?"

"Hi, Faith, sweetie. How are you doing?"

"As well as can be, I…."

"Everyone's worried about Y2K. It will be the year 2000, and Lord knows what's coming with our computers." Bernice paused, and her tone changed. "Wait, I hear birds. Are you at the cemetery again?" she scolded.

Exasperated, Faith sighed. "Yes."

"Honey, you need to come over and be with your family at a time like this."

"I *am* with my family," she spat.

"You know what I mean? Your cousins are here and we're cooking dinner. What you need is a good hot meal to keep your strength up."

"I'm not hungry. How can I eat when my mother can't?"

"I'm sorry. I didn't mean to upset you. I certainly don't want you to end up a character in one of your own novels. We're just concerned, don't cha know?"

Faith paused and took a deep breath to calm down. "I know. Besides, I hope Gina will get here for Christmas, so I won't be alone."

Her cousin persisted. "How is the house coming along, dear? It's going to be a bad time of the year to sell a house, you know. Why don't you keep it?"

"Mrs. Kravitz strikes again," mumbled Faith.

"What, sugar?"

Faith rolled her eyes. "Look, I'm sorry it doesn't make sense to you, but I already have a wonderful home and a great life. I'm used to being in the city now. I don't want to come back. Thanks for thinking of me, okay? Bye for now."

"But you should…"

She snapped her phone shut. "I *should*…"

She walked to a stone five markers away, pulled off her left glove, and touched her wedding ring. Surprisingly, it felt warm to the touch, a reminder of her husband's love.

She smiled.

"My love, I miss you. I'll never forget our first Christmas when I gave you a loaf of my home-made cinnamon bread. You were so impressed. Remember?"

Faith placed a flower in the thin metal vase attached to his stone and slipped her glove on. She paused for a minute and read the engraving.

Joseph Vyverberg
Husband – Father
Born: February 29, 1948
Died: February 14, 1994

She walked to another flat stone near two juniper trees and placed another flower. "Hello, Grandma Frances. Mom always brought me out here as a child. She wanted to show you the grandchild you never got to meet. I wish I had known you."

The sun briefly poked through the clouds and reflected off the ice on the stone.

Frances Flynn
January 17, 1901
October 17, 1950

She peered up at the sun. Its warmth made her happy.

She made her way to another stone in the row above. She used her key to break up the ice and brushed the slush from the marker.

"Hi, Great-Grandma Bridget. How many times I have looked at Grandma Frances' photo album and wondered what it would be like to meet you, to hear your voice. I've been walking in your footsteps at Mt. Hope for so long, I feel like I should know you."

She placed a poinsettia at the grave.

Bridget Shannon
1870 – 1935

Back home, Faith turned on the glistening Christmas tree in the corner of the living room. She pressed play on her reel-to-reel tape recorder and beautiful Christmas music of bell ringers accompanied by an organ filled the room. She looked up at a picture of her mother on the wall and burst into tears.

"I thought you would make it to Christmas, Mom." Overcome with grief, she fell to the floor in front of the tree, her body shaking with sobs.

The sun was setting on a dreary afternoon when Faith went to the refrigerator for a bite to eat. She wiped her tears with a tissue and blew her nose. She forced herself to eat something and drank a hot cup of Pero with milk.

Feeling a little brighter, she walked out the front door and turned on the porch lights wrapped with pine, holly garland, and red and green lights. The blowing wind made them sway. Everything looked so joyful, the exact opposite of how she was feeling.

Faith sighed and went back inside. She removed her mother's photo from the wall.

"I wanted to make everything so magical for you to the end, Mom. Just the way you made it special for me all those years."

She took the photo back to her chair and sat down.

Best of all, we got to do it twice, Mom. On December 6, St. Nicholas Day, we did the stockings. I always wished we had a fireplace to hang them on.

Instead, my stocking was under the tree, filled with little treats and small presents.

Faith looked around at three walls of the front room.

Four generations of my family lived here. I wonder how they celebrated Christmas. I like to imagine them here. Each one of them died in this house.

She looked to the right corner, where her mother's hospital bed had been so recently.

Mom died here in the front room, Grandma Frances in the living room, and Great-Grandma Bridget upstairs in her bedroom. The last two months of Great-Grandma Bridget's life she had the joy of holding her only grandchild, my mother.

"I feel guilty enjoying the lights without you, Mom."

She placed the eight by ten photo on the end table and walked over to her mother's hope chest. She grabbed the handle of the lower drawer and tried to pull it open, but discovered it was locked.

Faith opened the heavy lid and looked through the little compartments that folded out for the key.

No luck.

She found her grandmother's photo. Looking through the album always made her smile.

She picked up the handmade, neatly folded red, green, gold, and white quilt. Her grandmother had made it. She took them to the recliner, wrapped herself in the love of the quilt, and opened the old-fashioned photo album. Black sheets with silver corners filled the pages and were glued on the back to hold the photos in place.

There were only a few pictures of Great-Grandma Bridget. She was quite a lovely looking woman. Dainty, symmetrical features with her hair parted in the middle and drawn up into a braided bun. Tiny side curls framed her face. The plain black wedding dress was accented with ruffles, Juliet sleeves at the elbow, and a bustle.

She flipped the photo over and read, "Wedding 1875." Her Victorian black dress with its high collar and corset made her figure look like a supermodel. Faith yawned and lovingly surfed the next photo with her fingers. Written on the bottom in pencil, "1903". In the picture, Bridget sat in a chair while her children stood behind and around her. Faith especially noticed Iris, such a pretty little girl. Her grandmother Frances, a plump baby with long thick curls, sat on her lap. In another picture, Bridget was standing just a few feet from where Faith was now sitting.

Her eyelids were getting heavy, and she rested her eyes for a minute, then continued looking at the photos.

Studying the photo, Faith said to herself, "Wait, there's a Victorian door with etched glass behind her. I didn't know there was ever a door there." Curious, Faith picked up a crowbar from a toolbox and carefully punched a small hole in the old dry wall until she tapped on glass. She was careful not to break it.

"The door is still in the wall!" She continued chipping more drywall until the door was totally uncovered. When she placed her hands on the door's etched glass, light started to spread over it. She grabbed a hammer and pulled on some nails that were holding the door in the frame. Light was now bursting around the edges of the door.

How is that possible? It's 5:30 and dark outside.

Faith ran outside to look at the house where the door should be. The only light was coming from a streetlight and the glowing moon. Returning inside, the light was now brighter. She pushed on the door but was unable to open it. On the top left of the door, a key was hanging from a nail. She placed it in the keyhole and the door practically opened itself. She was looking at a tunnel that seemed to be made of clouds.

With trepidation, Faith stepped inside.

"I hope I don't fall through."

I have to have faith.

"Sleigh bells!" Excitement propelled her forward.

The sound came toward her. She was now in the front yard of the house, on the street that she grew up on. But it was *very* different. Across the street were farmland and a barn.

That wasn't there when I was a kid.

There were only a few houses on the street. The quaint streetlights were gas, and standing in the yard was an iron pump with a long handle above a well.

In the distance, she could hear the bells. They were coming from a handsome bay pulling a sleigh as it trotted down a short hill, dropped from view, then came around to the front of the house. The horse's bells were thrilling! The sleigh was filled with jolly people singing "Jingle Bells." They were bundled in furs, muffs, and high leather boots with buttons. It was like seeing in Ektachrome with rich saturated colors, and the snow softly glowing white from within.

Grandma Bridget exited the sleigh and put her foot on a two-step wooden box, then walked briskly toward Faith.

She looked back at the group and waved them on. "Come in. I have warm turkey, pies, and home-made cinnamon loaf," said Grandma. She looked at Faith lovingly like only a mother could, while everyone ran inside through the very door Faith had just discovered.

Faith was shocked. "Weird! Now I'm seeing the entire house as it was in Great-Grandma Bridget's time."

I soon realized that if you think of a place you want to go, suddenly you're there. Time is funny here. No one is aware I am here, only Great-Grandma.

Bridget made a plate of turkey, gravy, and mashed potatoes. Faith watched them pass the aromatic plates of food till one was placed before pretty Iris. Faith felt sad knowing Iris was not going to live much longer; she passed away at age seven. Great-Grandma didn't know this would be her last Christmas with Iris.

She sliced her big cinnamon loaf, just like what Faith's grandmother and mother made. She spread butter on each hot slice. Faith savored the cinnamon caramelized delight and imagined eating her own mother's bread.

Faith's thoughts drifted, and suddenly she was there, in the same kitchen, only in 1960.

"Whoa!" She felt a little dizzy from the fast time travel.

Great-Grandma Bridget grasped her arm and pointed to a kitchen wall. "There used to be a window there."

"I know. I found all kinds of windows in the walls. It made me think of you. I realized your hands had touched the windows endless times."

Grandma walked around the wall where the window used to be. She looked startled. "This used to be a porch."

"Well, Dad built a bathroom…"

Bridget's hands flew to her cheeks. "There's an outhouse in the house! Look at this porcelain tub. Where are the legs? We used a galvanized steel tub in the kitchen. So many changes." She shrugged. "Well, this house was always a work in progress. Grandpa and I dug out the basement and built the kitchen in 1891."

"The same year they put in the gas streetlamps. There was a story in the newspaper I found in that wall," said Faith excitedly.

"You found my memento," Great-Grandma said with gratitude. She smiled. "Victorians often put little mementos in the wall of their homes."

Grabbing Bridget's hand, Faith walked her back to the kitchen. She opened a door under the counter. "Some things never change. Look." She reached in for her large green bread bowl shaped like a basket.

Great-Grandma marveled at the treasure and lifted it from Faith's hands. "I made a lifetime of bread in this bowl," she stated emotionally.

Faith nodded. "Mom taught me how to make bread in this same bowl."

"Is that right?" Tears welled in her grey-blue eyes.

Thinking of Iris, Faith said, "I can't even imagine the trials you've been through in your life, Grandma."

"It wasn't easy, Faith. You have to keep your eyes on the horizon. Trust that in heaven's time, trials will work themselves out." She paused and seemed to study Faith's face. "We're all worried about you. All of us."

"All of whom?"

"Your family."

Puzzled, Faith asked, "How did this happen? You and me being together?"

"We can feel you through the veil, the ones who are tuned in. We can't see you, but we're aware." She paused. "You have the gift."

Great-Grandma pulled a watch from her pocket and flipped it open. She looked up. "I must go now."

Bridget grabbed her shawl and rushed out the door and across our modern yard. One she didn't belong in.

Faith followed behind. "Please don't leave, Grandma." Faith was feeling desperate. "Please, Great-Grandma."

Bridget glanced back. "You don't understand. We are quite busy, and I can't stay."

Faith screamed, "NO!"

Suddenly, she hit a clear wall at the curb of the street. She watched Great-Grandma Bridget walk into the evening sun of gold and amber, and she faded from her sight.

In panic, Faith screamed again, "GRANDMA!"

She abruptly sat up, and the photo album fell to the floor. She realized the tape reel had run out and was spinning round and round.

"What has just happened?"

Was Grandma just here?

The hair stood up on her arm, and she realized Great-Grandma was touching her, but the warmth of her presence was leaving.

She looked at the clock.

It's only 6:30.

It seemed to Faith that she was with Grandma Bridget for many days.

Feeling an intense loss, she paced the floor, trying to take in the meaning of this. She recalled their conversation; she never wanted to forget a word. It was so wonderful.

The phone rang startling Faith. She flipped it open; it was her daughter. She pushed accept.

"Hi, Gina. I'm glad you called. You won't believe what just happened to me."

"Mom, you'll have to tell me later. Rob just got off work, and we hope to come and spend Christmas with you. Chicago is crazy. We decided to rent a car, everyone is worried about Y2K and panicking. They're claiming time is going to crash soon."

Suddenly, Faith felt relief from her loneliness. "It's wonderful news you're coming. What a surprise. I have the kids' presents here under the tree, and I made them a little tent."

"Are you still selling the house? I'm going to be so sad to not be able to come home anymore," Gina lamented.

Faith glanced down at the bread bowl shelf. "Yes, I'm working away! Made a lot of progress, but there are tools and messes everywhere."

"Sorry, Mom. We just got to the car rental, so I have to go now. Talk to you later. Oh, Bernice called. She wants to see the kids and invited us to Christmas dinner tomorrow night."

"Okay, I'll see you soon. Drive safe."

Faith pulled Grandma Bridget's bread bowl off the shelf. She poured water from the teapot into the bowl, added sugar, and sprinkled yeast across the water.

She glanced up. The wall where the old door had been was undisturbed.

"Am I going crazy?" She rubbed her forehead with her fingers. No, she was here.

Faith cleaned up the tools from the floor to make it safe for the children. She turned on the TV and watched a choir singing Christmas carols. She added flour, sugar, and kneaded the bread, then covered it with a towel.

She went under the stairway and pulled out a box of old ornaments, remnants from her childhood. She set the box on an end table near her chair and hung up her mother's photo.

She turned off the TV, turned on her Christmas music, and massaged her aching legs. She turned off the overhead lights and made her way to the recliner. Faith put her legs up and looked around at the Christmas lights with satisfaction. She covered herself with the quilt and smiled at the tree.

It's just like Mom would have done.

She lifted the box of ornaments to her lap, shuffled through them, and found a red glass globe with white flocking. It read, *Merry Christmas Faith.* It had been for her first Christmas.

Slowly, her eyes felt heavy, and she placed the cherry orb precariously on the end table. She leaned back, lost in choir music as she dozed off.

Her thoughts drifted to the cemetery, and it was cold. Half asleep, she pulled Grandma Franny's quilt closer.

Straight ahead are the two tall juniper trees that form an arch. Faith walked between the trees and unexpectedly stepped on a stone. She wiped the snow from it, to see it was her grandma Frances' grave.

Faith looked up to see a glowing white tunnel in front of her. She stepped inside, and at the end, found an old cellar door with peeling red paint.

Light peered from the cracks. "This is strange. Why is there a cellar door here?"

She pulled the handle and opened the door. Carefully, she walked down some stairs to the dirt floor.

I recognize this place. It's our basement.

The only light came from a funny narrow window about one foot by two feet.

As a child, I was always intrigued by that window.

A woman's voice came from behind Faith. "Do you know what that is?"

Faith nearly jumped out of her skin.

She turned to see a woman. "How did you get here?"

"It's my house," said the woman.

"What? It's my mother's house. She lived here."

The woman looked around the basement like it was an old friend as the window shined a ray of light on the older woman's face.

Suddenly, Faith realized who she was. "Grandma Frances?"

"Yes, Faith."

"Now, how do you know my name?"

The old woman slipped the hood off her grey hair. She seemed to glow from inside, and the basement filled with light. Faith felt a deep sense of relief, and all her sadness left.

"I don't have long, but I wanted to see you. I sensed you were seeking relief. It occurred to me you may be looking at my photo album. When you touch things that belonged to your loved ones, it creates powerful feelings," explained Grandma Frances.

"We never got to meet. You passed before I could know you. You're like I imagined you though, from your photo."

"Heaven is all around you," she imparted with tenderness.

Faith wondered what that meant, but her mind quickly darted to something she wanted her grandmother to know.

"Whenever I searched in the old newspapers, it was so rewarding to find your name. You felt real to me." Faith stared at the odd-sized window with curiosity. "So, tell me what is that window for? Then there's that metal thing that looks sort of like a slide."

Frances laughed. "It's a coal chute. The men would pour the coal through the window, and it would fall into a large box down at the bottom of the chute. Then we children would come down with a bucket to get coal for the oven upstairs."

"That's so weird. Isn't coal what bad children got in their stockings?"

"No, silly. During the depression, families couldn't afford coal. The poor like us would send our children down to the train tracks in winter. They would pick up chunks of coal that fell next to the train on the ground while workers were unloading. Sometimes the fireman on the train would take pity on the children and, with his oversized shovel, threw it out to us for fun. We laughed and laughed. It was such a game to see who could get the most. In Turkey, for St. Nick's time, he gave the children coal in their shoes to keep them warm."

"Really? I never considered that. What was your Christmas like?"

"We didn't have much. But one year, I made your mother a doll, the little clothes, and a small quilt. Then I took a Quaker's oatmeal box, cut a hole in the side, and made a cradle out of it. I glued tissue paper all around the cradle."

"Mom told me about that. She said it was her favorite toy. In fact, I found it in the hope chest. It's lovely, and every stitch is perfect. So much love went into that. We always celebrated St. Nicholas Day like you did.

"I asked Mom how St. Nicholas could come to our house because we didn't have a fireplace. She said the chimney in the kitchen had a door in the basement."

Faith grabbed her grandmother's arm and led her to the chimney. "Look at that door. It's about eight-inch square. How can St. Nick get through there?"

Grandma laughed. "He's magic. I told your mother, Regina, the same thing!"

"Really?"

Now they both laughed.

"Oh, Grandma Franny. You're making me feel like Mom is here. You're so much alike." Faith marveled.

"Give me your hand."

Grandma took Faith's hand, and in one blink, they stood in the kitchen. Being a mere mortal, Faith, of course, lost her balance,

Grandma looked around and walked to the bread bowl cabinet. "Oh, my bread bowl is still here, and my mother's is, too."

"That's how Mom kept you near to her. Mom and I used to make bread with both of the bowls, and she'd tell me they were yours and Great-Grandma Bridget's. I felt you were there every time we kneaded the bread."

Grandma Frances touched Faith's face and pushed the hair back off her eyes. "I always wondered what you would grow up to be. I'm so impressed."

They linked arms and walked into the living room where the Christmas tree was.

"How lovely. Did you decorate this?" Grandma Frances admired the festive tree. Her eyes moved down to the base, and Faith noticed she spied the crèche. "My nativity, made in Italy."

Faith nodded. "That's right, it is."

"Yes, my last Christmas with Regina we went to Lancaster to buy it. Your mother just loved it."

"Me, too. It's painted so beautifully."

So that's how you decorated.

"Let's look at your photo album. I have so many questions," said Faith.

"I cannot, my dear." She turned to walk away.

Faith asked firmly, "How is Mom?"

"It's getting late, and St. Nicholas will come soon." Grandma Frances chuckled.

She picked up an old Bible from the open hope chest and handed it to me. "Merry Christmas, my dear. My father gave this to me on Christmas Eve years ago."

Faith took it and held it close to her chest.

A bright light burned above her grandma; small at first, but then it grew and the entire room lit up. Light poured from within her, a beautiful smile covered her face, and her eyes twinkled.

Faith was surrounded by light as Grandma disappeared into it. She heard indescribable heavenly music that seemed to be angels singing, and she felt inadequate.

She felt her grandma's warmth leave the room, and she called out for her not to go, but to no avail.

Faith was anxious and didn't want to be abandoned. Nearby footsteps woke her up, and she realized she wasn't alone.

"Mother?" Faith waved her arms around. She heard glass shatter and jumped up. The old Bible fell off her lap and hit the floor with a splat.

Oh no, my childhood ornament is broken!

"Who are you?" she demanded.

The intruder turned around and surprised Faith.

She could tell by his long white beard, green velvet cape, and black boots, that it was Old St. Nick.

He winked. "Now, no need to panic! It's just me."

"Did you come through the chimney?"

"Yes. If you must know." He brushed the black soot off his sleeves. "It was a tight fit." He looked right at her. "You're still a disbeliever, I see."

Faith frowned. "I hoped you were my mother."

"I'm terribly sorry to disappoint you."

She looked down at the shattered keepsake on the floor and started to cry.

"Oh, no!"

"It's just a material thing, Faith. You have so much more."

She stopped crying and looked at him. "You're right, St. Nick. No one should know better than you."

She watched him carefully add some small presents into her childhood stocking.

"Watching you gives me a comforting feeling. So, it is true about you. Putting presents in children's shoes and stockings."

"Yes. The scriptures say charity is the pure love of God, Faith. I'm just an extension of God's love. So are you. Look at your bird feeder. The cardinals and squirrels are feeling your love for them. Love is all we take with us. By and by, in a twinkle, we will all be together again."

He walked over to Faith and put his leather gloved hand on her shoulder. "Your mother misses you, too." He laid her stocking under the tree and winked his azure eye at her. "I must take my leave."

"For crying out loud. Why are you all in such a hurry?"

"The sun arises." He set his finger beside his nose. A familiar glowing light came from within him. He smiled as he dissolved into another dimension.

Faith tingled all over, just like that first time when Santa came. It was magic.

"Heaven is all around us," Grandma Franny had said.

The sun's first light was coming up over the horizon. Faith barely saw his sleigh streak across the sky ahead of the light.

She slept on the couch until a light warmed her face. She woke thinking about all the things that happened last night. Each visit was a treasured memory. Her childhood dream was to meet St. Nicholas, that jolly elf of love.

Why would he come to me?

Then she noticed her ornament was not broken on the floor.

That's strange. Did I imagine that?

She picked up her old stocking. She looked inside to find some candies and nuts. Then a little present. She ripped off the paper and bow. It couldn't be. It was the little horse picture her mother had given her as a child. Just three by five inches with a gold frame. It was her favorite, and she was overcome with emotion.

Next, she found a green box with a tiny clear plastic deer set inside, small and delicate. Her mother had bought these for her, and she loved them. Back then, she had taken them to the backyard and played with them in the grass. They were so small that she lost them. It broke her heart because she loved them so.

Kneeling in the grass, Faith had looked all day, but she didn't find them. Her mother must have known how badly she had felt about it.

She looked again. There was one more wrapped present.

"What's in here?"

Faith unfolded the tissue paper. "My special ornament! It's fixed!" A mother's love can fix anything. She started to cry, picked it up by the hook, and hung it on the tree.

My precious gem.

She dropped the stocking, and it hit the floor with a light thump. Thinking there must be something heavy in there, she picked it up and reached all the way to down to the bottom. There was a key.

"Thank you, Mom," she whispered.

She inserted it in the bottom drawer of the hope chest, turned the key, and pulled open the memory drawer. It was filled with her writings and drawings from childhood. She remembered her mother lovingly put them there for safekeeping.

She laughed when she saw the construction paper banjo she had made. It had natural colored yarn threaded with gold tinsel for strings. She thought it was a masterpiece.

Church bells played "Joy to the World." Christmas had come and so had the women who loved Faith.

Just then, Gina and her family pulled up in their SUV.

Faith ran to greet them.

"You won't believe the night I had."

"You'll have to tell me about it, Mom," said Gina.

"Hi, Mom." Her son-in-law Jake gave her a hug.

"I made some cinnamon loaf last night. Would you like some?"

Jake smiled. "I can't wait to spread melted butter all over it. The way to a man's heart is through his stomach."

They all laughed.

Faith hugged her sleepy grandchildren, and they screamed for joy at all the presents under the tree.

Gina looked into her mother's eyes with compassion. "I can't believe you got all this done. We sure appreciate it, Mom. How are you holding up?"

"I'm good now that you're here."

After a few presents were opened, Gina and Jake yawned. "Can we get this couch bed ready, Mom? We're tired."

"It's all ready for you."

Jake looked over the tent his mother-in-law had put up earlier. "Mom, this fairy tent is precious."

He turned to his children. "You kids want to go into the tent and get some sleep?"

They piled in, and Jake helped the two youngest into their sleeping bags. Six-year-old Heather played with her new fashion doll. Faith offered Heather a bite of Grandma's bread.

Faith's hand gently wiped the dust from the top of her laptop. She opened it and pushed the on button.

Faith began typing: *Three generations, the matriarchs of the Flynn family, had touched her life in so many ways. The bread bowls will always stay on the same shelf just as they had been. More generations will feel the magic that she did in this house. More husbands like her Joseph will fall in love by eating homemade cinnamon bread.*

Faith laughed to herself.

I guess those pioneers left a blessing to us all,

calling this place Mt. Hope. I'm not selling this house. It belongs to our family.

Her mom always said, "Use your imagination, Faith. You are only limited in heaven by the lack of creativity you express here on earth. Dream with all your might."

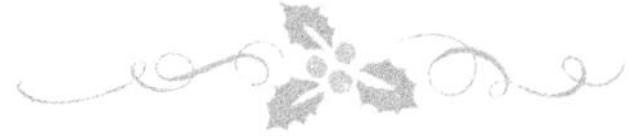

Faith typed on a new page. *Heaven's Time.*

Her heart stopped hurting; she no longer felt survivor's guilt. That St. Nick was a gifted old elf to read her sad heart. Then she realized Mom had sent St. Nicholas. She had always believed in his example so much.

Nicholas must have dreamed while on earth that he could come back to make children happy for eternity. She felt she was her mother's eternity.

Faith looked at the old crèche under the tree. She walked over and touched the baby Jesus. Heather joined her touching the oxen, the sheep, and then Jesus in the manger.

Great-Grandma Franny," said Heather ly.

Faith looked surprised. "But you didn't know her."

"Yes, I do. She came to me in the car. We talked and then she said she had to go home. I said that's funny, because Mommy said we're going home, too."

Faith paused in wonder. "Yes, you've come home, my love."

She pulled Heather to her, and they held each other close.

THE END

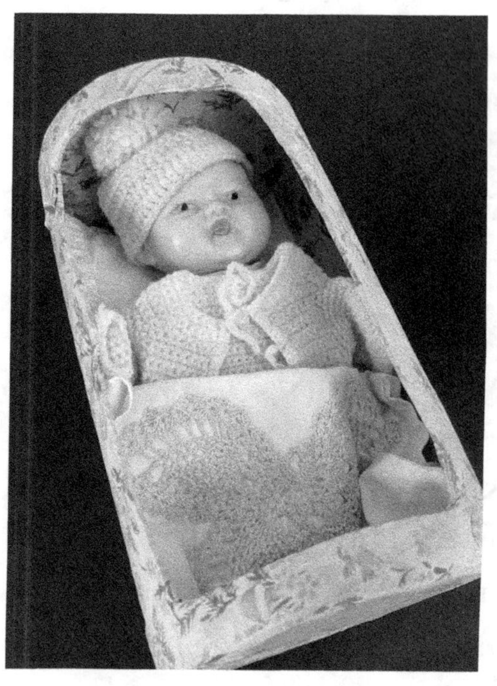

My grandmother Mary Cecelia Rooney died of cancer weeks before my parents got married in November of 1952. She was waiting for my dad to come home from Korea to marry mom. She lovingly made this doll for my mom in about 1936. My mother always told me it was her favorite Christmas present.

People always ask—what inspired you to write this story. There is rarely one motivation, but this photo was an important one. The matriarch is Mary Ann Rooney, my great-grandmother. The child in her lap is Mary Cecelia, and the young girl on the far left is Francine (Iris.) She did not live another year. In the local newpaper, her obituary stated that she had died of an illness and that her classmates had carried her coffin. If they had only had antibiotics.

Acknowledgments

My FIRST THANK YOU will always be to Richard Paul Evans and his Author Ready program.

Next, I want to thank Debbie Ihler Rasmussen for making me look better than I am! Where would we be without content editors? Yikes!

Wyvanna Hood was my cover artist. She has such a great talent, and I appreciate her so much. Thank you.

We have the best team Author Ready. Kim Autrey is a kind and detailed professional who copyedited my work. Thanks so much Kim.

Francine Platt is equally talented and artistic with my inside formatting and artwork. I know I can trust her with anything I do. Thanks Francine.

I also want to thank my sister Karen. She is my greatest supporter. Always asking how my song or writing is coming. I appreciate it more than she will ever know.

Lastly, I want to thank my brother Butch. He too, has always followed my efforts with great love and care, and this will be the last time I will ever say that. But I'm sure he knows somehow in heaven that his sister is improving herself.

ABOUT THE AUTHOR

Patricia M Boardman is genealogist, writer, historian and actress.

A lifelong genealogist she turned to history to understand the story of her ancestors once the documents revealed all they could. Her passion covers many aspects of history. "Under every tombstone is a story" is her motto. She is from Dubuque, Iowa but has lived in Southern California for the last 37 years.

Patricia created the Pint-Size Pioneer Program for elementary school children to teach history and good citizenship. She served on the board of the Santa Ana Historical Preservation Society where she wrote, directed several historic cemetery tours educate the public. She also published a book for the Orange County Cemetery District called *Remember Me: Mini-biographies of Pioneers Buried in the Santa Ana Cemetery*—a self-guided historic tour of the Santa Ana Cemetery with map.

The author is a mother of four and grandmother of eight.

Contact Patricia at pmboardmanauthor@gmail.com or at facebook.com/pmboardmanauthor.